Look at a Maple Tree

by Patricia M. Stockland

Lerner Publications Company · Minneapolis

This is a root of a maple tree.

This is a trunk of a maple tree.

This is a branch of a maple tree.

This is a leaf of a
maple tree.

This is a seed of a maple tree.

This is a maple tree!

The images in this book are used with the permission of: © Igor Kisselev/Shutterstock.com, p. 2; © Brykaylo Yuriy/Shutterstock.com, p. 3; © TonyP_Images/Alamy, p. 4; © Taylor S. Kennedy/National Geographic RF/Glow Images, p. 5; © Carol Sharp/Flowerphotos/Glow Images, p. 6; © Flashon Studio/Dreamstime.com, p. 7.
Front cover: © Adam Jones/Photodisc/Getty Images.

Lerner Publications Company
A division of Lerner Publishing Group, Inc.
241 First Avenue North
Minneapolis, MN 55401 U.S.A.

Website address: www.lernerbooks.com

Main body text set in ITC Avant Garde Gothic Std 21/25.
Typeface provided by International Typeface Corp.

Library of Congress Cataloging-in-Publication Data

Stockland, Patricia M.
Look at a maple tree / by Patricia M. Stockland.
p. cm. — (First step nonfiction. Look at trees)
Maple tree
ISBN 978–1–4677–0522–6 (pbk. : alk. paper)
1. Maple—Juvenile literature. I. Title. II. Title: Maple tree. III. Series: Stockland, Patricia M. First step nonfiction. Look at trees.
SD397.M3S76 2013
583'.78—dc23 2012013241

Manufactured in the United States of America
1 – BP – 7/15/12